The TORTOISE and the HARE

Retold by BLAKE HOENA
Illustrations by TIM PALIN
Music by ERIK KOSKINEN

CANTATA
LEARNING

WWW.CANTATALEARNING.COM

CANTATA LEARNING

Published by Cantata Learning
1710 Roe Crest Drive
North Mankato, MN 56003
www.cantatalearning.com

Library of Congress Cataloging-in-Publication Data
Names: Hoena, B. A., author. | Palin, Tim, illustrator. | Koskinen, Erik,
    composer. | Aesop.
Title: The tortoise and the hare / retold by Blake Hoena ; illustrated by Tim
    Palin ; music by Erik Koskinen.
Description: North Mankato, MN : Cantata Learning, [2018] | Series: Classic
    fables in rhythm and rhyme | Summary: A modern song retells the events of
    the famous race between the boastful hare and the persevering tortoise.
    Includes a brief introduction to Aesop, sheet music, glossary, discussion
    questions, and further reading.
Identifiers: LCCN 2017017531 (print) | LCCN 2017035538 (ebook) | ISBN
    9781684101740 (ebook) | ISBN 9781684101344 (hardcover : alk. paper) | ISBN
    9781684101887 (paperback : alk. paper)
Subjects: | CYAC: Behavior--Songs and music. | Fables. | Folklore. | Songs.
Classification: LCC PZ8.3.H667 (ebook) | LCC PZ8.3.H667 Tor 2018 (print) |
    DDC 398.2 [E] --dc23
LC record available at https://lccn.loc.gov/2017017531

Book design and art direction, Tim Palin Creative
Editorial direction, Kellie M. Hultgren
Music direction, Elizabeth Draper
Music arranged and produced by Erik Koskinen

Printed in the United States of America in North Mankato, Minnesota.
122017   0378CGS18

ACCESS THE MUSIC!

SCAN CODE WITH MOBILE APP

CANTATALEARNING.COM

TIPS TO SUPPORT LITERACY AT HOME

WHY READING AND SINGING WITH YOUR CHILD IS SO IMPORTANT

Daily reading with your child leads to increased academic achievement. Music and songs, specifically rhyming songs, are a fun and easy way to build early literacy and language development. Music skills correlate significantly with both phonological awareness and reading development. Singing helps build vocabulary and speech development. And reading and appreciating music together is a wonderful way to strengthen your relationship.

READ AND SING EVERY DAY!

TIPS FOR USING CANTATA LEARNING BOOKS AND SONGS DURING YOUR DAILY STORY TIME

1. As you sing and read, point out the different words on the page that rhyme. Suggest other words that rhyme.

2. Memorize simple rhymes such as Itsy Bitsy Spider and sing them together. This encourages comprehension skills and early literacy skills.

3. Use the questions in the back of each book to guide your singing and storytelling.

4. Read the included sheet music with your child while you listen to the song. How do the music notes correlate to the words of the song?

5. Sing along on the go and at home. Access music by scanning the QR code on each Cantata book. You can also stream or download the music for free to your computer, smartphone, or mobile device.

Devoting time to daily reading shows that you are available for your child. Together, you are building language, literacy, and listening skills.

Have fun reading and singing!

Aesop was a storyteller who wrote hundreds of stories called **fables**. These short tales often had animals for characters. Each story is meant to teach a **moral**, or lesson.

In this fable, there is a speedy **hare**, or rabbit. There is also a slow but steady **tortoise**, or turtle. What lesson can be learned from the tortoise and the hare?

Turn the page to find out. Remember to sing along!

There was a speedy rabbit,
who **bragged** how fast he ran.

He sped right up to the top of a hill,
and he zoomed back down again.

Oh, the rabbit bragged he was fast.
He told everyone with glee,
"When I run as fast as I can,
no one can catch me."

There was a **pokey** turtle
with a slow and steady pace.

He was tired of all the rabbit's **boasts**,
so he challenged him to a race.

The rabbit started off fast.
The turtle was slow and steady.

The rabbit looked back and began to laugh, "You'll never catch up to me."

The rabbit was far ahead,
so he thought he could relax.

As the turtle kept going, steady and slow, that rabbit took a nap.

When the rabbit woke, it was late.

The turtle was about to win.

The rabbit took off as fast as he could
but couldn't catch up to him.

All the other animals cheered
as the turtle won the race.

That bragging rabbit could not beat
his slow and steady pace.

So you can brag about your skills,
but remember this moral too:
Success comes not from what you say
but how your talents are used!

Success comes not from what you say
but how your talents are used!

SONG LYRICS
The Tortoise and the Hare

There was a speedy rabbit,
who bragged how fast he ran.
He sped right up to the top of a hill,
and he zoomed back down again.

Oh, the rabbit bragged he was fast.
He told everyone with glee,
"When I run as fast as I can,
no one can catch me."

There was a pokey turtle
with a slow and steady pace.
He was tired of all the rabbit's boasts,
so he challenged him to a race.

The rabbit started off fast.
The turtle was slow and steady.
The rabbit looked back and began to laugh,
"You'll never catch up to me."

The rabbit was far ahead,
so he thought he could relax.
As the turtle kept going, steady and slow,
that rabbit took a nap.

When the rabbit woke, it was late.
The turtle was about to win.
The rabbit took off as fast as he could
but couldn't catch up to him.

All the other animals cheered
as the turtle won the race.
That bragging rabbit could not beat
his slow and steady pace.

So you can brag about your skills,
but remember this moral too:
Success comes not from what you say
but how your talents are used!

Success comes not from what you say
but how your talents are used!

The Tortoise and the Hare

Americana
Erik Koskinen

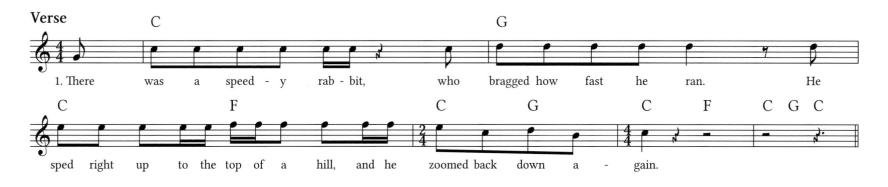

Verse

1. There was a speed-y rab-bit, who bragged how fast he ran. He sped right up to the top of a hill, and he zoomed back down a-gain.

Verse 2
Oh, the rabbit bragged he was fast.
He told everyone with glee,
"When I run as fast as I can,
no one can catch me."

Verse 3
There was a pokey turtle
with a slow and steady pace.
He was tired of all the rabbit's boasts,
so he challenged him to a race.

Verse 4
The rabbit started off fast.
The turtle was slow and steady.
The rabbit looked back and began to laugh,
"You'll never catch up to me."

Verse 5
The rabbit was far ahead,
so he thought he could relax.
As the turtle kept going, steady and slow,
that rabbit took a nap.

Verse 6
When the rabbit woke, it was late.
The turtle was about to win.
The rabbit took off as fast as he could
but couldn't catch up to him.

Verse 7
All the other animals cheered
as the turtle won the race.
That bragging rabbit could not beat
his slow and steady pace.

Outro

So you can brag a-bout your skills, but re-mem-ber this mor-al too: Suc-cess comes not from what you say but how your tal-ents are used! how your tal-ents are used!

GLOSSARY

Aesop—a legendary storyteller who is said to have lived in ancient Greece around 600 BCE

boasts—proud claims that are bigger than reality

bragged—talked very proudly about something

fables—short stories that often have animal characters and teach a lesson

hare—a large kind of rabbit

moral—a lesson, often found in a fable or story

pokey—slow

tortoise—turtle

GUIDED READING ACTIVITIES

1. The rabbit is good at running really fast, and the turtle is good at keeping a steady pace. What is something that you are good at?

2. What are some things that it is best to do fast? What are some things that is better to do slow?

3. Do you feel you are more like the tortoise or the hare? Why?

4. Which is your favorite animal, the tortoise or the hare? Draw a picture of it!

TO LEARN MORE

Hoena, Blake. *The Fox and the Grapes*. North Mankato, MN: Cantata Learning, 2018.

Ian, Nicholas. *The Grand Old Duke of York*. North Mankato, MN: Cantata Learning, 2016.

Pinkney, Jerry. *The Tortoise and the Hare*. New York: Little, Brown Books for Young Readers, 2013.

West, David. *Ten of the Best Animal Myths*. New York: Crabtree, 2015.